GIRLS SURVIVE

Published by Stone Arch Books, an imprint of Capstone.
1710 Roe Crest Drive, North Mankato, Minnesota 56003
capstonepub.com

Library of Congress Cataloging-in-Publication Data is available on the
Library of Congress website
ISBN: 9781666340754 (hardcover)
ISBN: 9781666340792 (paperback)
ISBN: 9781666340808 (ebook PDF)

Summary: In 1935, dust storms are sweeping across the southern plains of the
United States, including Oklahoma. Twelve-year-old Millie Horn is worried about
her family's survival. The Dust Bowl is getting worse, and her family is running out
of food and money. Despite the hardships, Pa doesn't want to abandon the farm,
which has been in the family for generations. But when the worst "black blizzard"
yet hits, they have no choice. The family decides to make the journey west, but life
in California isn't without struggle. Can Millie and her family survive the Dust
Bowl and the hardships of the Great Depression?

Editorial Credits
Editor: Alison Deering; Designer: Sarah Bennett;
Production Specialist: Katy LaVigne

Design Elements
Shutterstock: Max Lashcheuski (background texture),
Olena Rodina (background pattern)

Printed and bound in the USA. 4882

MILLIE
AND THE
GREAT DROUGHT

A Dust Bowl
Survival Story

by Natasha Deen

illustrated by Wendy Tan

STONE ARCH BOOKS
a capstone imprint

CHAPTER ONE

"Hurry, Millie!" Pa called. "Come see the plants!"

I headed from our house to the fields. The spring breeze made me shiver. Ever since the dust storms started four years ago, all I felt was cold.

"The potatoes are growing!" Pa stroked the delicate green shoots. "This is going to be our year."

"I'm sure you're right," I said, not believing a word.

Pa laughed. His brown eyes crinkled. "Have some faith. Potatoes are a new crop, but I can do it."

I didn't doubt Pa's skills. Our farm had been in his family since my great-great-grandfather. Farming was in our blood.

What I doubted was the rain.

Oklahoma never got a lot of rain, but the past four years had brought drought conditions. The humming wind that used to bring moisture now brought stinging dust storms.

Last year, my best friend, Betty Adams, and I had tried counting how many storms hit our county. After the thirty-third, we stopped counting. It was too sad to keep going.

To make matters worse, we were in the middle of the Great Depression. I didn't exactly understand what it was, except it meant the price of wheat had dropped. That's why Pa was growing potatoes this year. He hoped the crop would return our farm to old times.

But it was hard to keep hoping.

"Think of it, my girl," Pa said, bringing my attention back to him. "When this crop sells, we won't need the government to give us food. We'll be independent again."

My eyes misted at the longing in Pa's voice. I knew it was hard for him to accept help, but the storms gave us no choice. They were unlike anything anyone had ever experienced. They suffocated people and livestock, including our cows and chickens.

When it was late and dark, I cried over our lost animals. I did it quietly, so my parents wouldn't hear and worry.

"It's not so bad, accepting help, is it?" I asked.

Pa shook his head. "The government can't always step in. Folks need gumption to get them through difficult times."

I looked east to where the Johnson farm sat. Effort and a good attitude hadn't helped them.

Six weeks ago, Mr. Johnson had died from dust pneumonia. His family had been forced to leave their land and migrate to California.

"Pa . . . ," I paused. "The Johnsons moved because of the drought. Have you—" I could hardly get the words out. "Maybe we should do the same? Ma says so."

I think we should too, I wanted to add. But it took all my courage just to ask the question.

"Millie." Pa puffed out a shallow breath. "They had to leave. Mrs. Johnson couldn't keep up with the farmwork on her own. I'm not going anywhere, I promise."

"You can't know that," I protested.

Pa knelt next to me. "This farm isn't going anywhere and neither am I," he said firmly. "Tough times come and go. Before you were born—heck, before *I* was born—there was a terrible drought. But my family made it through. We're going to be fine. We have the new crop. Remember what we always say?"

"'Till the soil, and the rain will come,'" I said, echoing Pa's words.

But I didn't trust those words—not anymore. Everyone in our county had been tilling the soil—cutting down trees and grass to make way for wheat fields—but rain hadn't come.

"This farm will be here for your great-grandchildren. I promise." Pa squeezed my hand and rose to his feet. "Come on, let's get back for supper."

I followed Pa from the field. In the distance was our farmhouse. We used to have a red roof and white curtains. But after years of storms, the paint had been blasted away, and our curtains were no longer white. Ma would wash them until they shone. Then a storm would hit, and the brilliant white would turn gray-black with dust.

Ma kept cleaning, and the storms kept coming. I wondered why she kept trying.

As Pa and I made our way back toward the farmhouse, I saw it—the growing darkness in the sky. Static electricity jittered along my skin. My heart jittered too.

"Pa—" I started.

"I see it," Pa said tightly. "Quickly, now." He steered me toward the cellar.

We picked up our pace, but the storm was faster than our feet.

"Run, Millie!" Pa cried. He grabbed my hand and pulled me along with him as the black cloud rolled our way.

"Ma!" I screamed. "Take cover!"

I sped for the cellar door, but it was hard to see anything. Dust stung my face and exposed skin. Overhead, the sky grew dark, the sun disappeared, and the storm descended with its full might.

CHAPTER TWO

My legs pumped—harder, faster—to get me to safety. Through the swirling storm, I saw Ma at the cellar, fighting to keep the door open.

"Come on!" she cried. "Quickly!"

I raced down the steps. Pa took the door from Ma and locked it tight behind us, shutting out the storm and sealing us in.

Inside the cellar, my parents were shadowy figures. I sat on the bench that ran along one of the walls. The other side was lined with shelves that used to hold food but were now empty.

Outside, the storm raged. The noise drilled into my body and burrowed into my bones.

Tornadoes sounded like freight trains when they hurled their fury across the plains. But these storms wailed like a blizzard.

My skin started to itch, like there were thousands of insects scurrying along my arms. My insides felt itchy too, and I fought to stay calm. Ma and Pa had enough on their minds without worrying about me. Not that they could see me in the dim light. With the storm whining overhead, maybe they wouldn't even hear me panicking.

But I'd know, and I didn't like that. I needed to be like Ma and Pa. Strong. Calm. Determined to see the storm through.

I concentrated on staying motionless. I hoped this storm would last minutes instead of hours. I hoped Pa was right about this year's crop.

I shut my eyes. I was tired of hoping.

After what felt like hours, it suddenly went quiet outside. When the silence stayed and Pa was sure the storm was over, he shuffled to the cellar door. His footsteps swished against the dirt floor.

I heard the lock disengage. Pa grunted, and the door creaked open. A sliver of light snuck through the crack.

Pa grunted again and pushed. Dirt and daylight spilled into the cellar.

Ma and Pa climbed out. I hung back, fearful of the destruction on the other side.

"Come along, Millie," said Ma, "before dinner gets cold." There was a beat of silence, then, "Before dinner gets colder."

I took a breath, but my chest stayed tight.

"Millie!"

I jumped at Pa's voice and stumbled out of the cellar. Outside, everything was covered in gray dust.

I'd learned to tell where the storm had come from based on the color of the dust. Here, our dust was red. But other states were struggling with the storms too. Brown dirt came from Kansas. Gray dust meant this storm had blown in from Colorado or New Mexico.

Pa glanced over to the field. His jaw clenched at the sight of the buried potato shoots he'd been admiring earlier. But when he looked my way, he forced a smile. "Let's see what's on the table tonight!"

Dirt, I thought. *Dirt is on the table.*

It wouldn't matter that Ma had covered the food with a tablecloth. The dust and sand got *everywhere*. It blew in through the cracks in the walls and trickled down from the roof.

Back at the house, we brushed dust off the table, chairs, and food. I forced myself to sit and eat. The Great Depression was hitting every American hard. Food was so scarce that the government had taken to handing out rations. I couldn't waste dinner, even if the bread crunched with sand and there was dirt in the beef.

After dinner, I tidied up while Ma and Pa went to sit on the back porch. I did my best, but no amount of sweeping got rid of the dust. It even coated my skin.

As I bent to toss the rubbish into the bin, my parents' voices drifted inside. I could tell from their low tones that they didn't want me to hear what they were saying. Setting the broom aside, I crept to the back door and listened.

"It's time, John," Ma said. "I can't stand it anymore! Our house is never clean. We're never clean. I'm tired of dirt in my food!"

"Don't be like that," Pa soothed. "We've been through rough times before."

"Not like this!" Ma's voice cracked. "We're relying on the government for food. The animals are gone. The neighbors are gone!"

"I'm sorry they didn't want to stick it out," Pa said, his tone flat. "But I'm not leaving. This is our home. If it rains, the crops will recover. If not, next year—"

"Next year," Ma spat at him. "If you're not jawing about the rain, you're promising next year will be better. Except it's not. Everything is getting worse!"

I blinked back the tears. This wasn't a new fight. My parents had been arguing about selling the farm for more than a year.

"We need to leave," Ma insisted. "The prices of wheat keep dropping—twenty-three cents per bushel!"

"That's why we're planting potatoes," Pa argued. "They're a hardier crop. They'll sell for more. If that doesn't work, we'll try turnips."

I leaned closer, and the board under me let out a loud *creak*. Ma and Pa went quiet.

I walked away, making sure the board creaked again so they'd think I left. After a moment, I snuck back to my spot.

"If we wait much longer, we won't have enough money to make the move to California," Ma said, her words thick with tears. She had dropped her voice, but I still heard her. "We'll be stuck here."

Tears clogged my throat too. I loved the farm as much as Pa, but Ma was right. We needed to leave. No matter what Pa said, the crops couldn't grow without the rain. Every day, more folks left.

"This land's always had hardships," Pa argued. "And my family always got through them. We'll get through this."

"These storms are different," Ma said. "They don't stop."

The fear in her voice terrified me. Ma was one of the strongest people I knew. If she was scared, what hope was there?

"This year, Mary," Pa said, "We'll see a reverse in our fortunes. I promise."

If I were brave, I'd have burst through the door and told Pa the truth. That we had to leave. That I agreed with Ma. That I was worried too.

But it was hard to stay brave when Pa was so sad. Every time Ma brought up leaving the farm, he shut down or walked away.

I crept away from the door and headed to bed, feeling like a coward. Maybe tomorrow I'd find my bravery and tell Pa how I felt. Maybe tomorrow the storms would be gone.

Maybe. But I doubted it.

CHAPTER THREE

I sat on the wooden bench outside the school
doors and waited for my friend Betty. She was a
year older than me, but because of the storms and
people moving, all the grades were taught in the
same room. My class only had eight students.

I kicked my feet, watching the sky. Dust storms
could come at any time.

A moment later, Betty stepped outside.

"Here," she said. Her blond curls bounced as she
sat beside me. "I brought you these." She dropped a

handful of caramel cubes into my palm. "No one's buying candy. Dad said I could bring some to share with you."

Betty's father, Mr. Adams, owned the general store. It was kind of them to share the candy, but the caramels felt heavy in my hand.

"No, I can't," I said.

I tried to swallow the lump lodged in my throat. The food Ma and Pa received from the government was enough to feed us, but it wasn't enough to share.

"I don't have anything I can trade you," I explained.

"They're for you," Betty repeated, a catch in her voice. She pushed my hand to my chest. "Millie—" She shook her head, as if trying to clear her thoughts. "Take them, please. From me?"

I hesitated, then put the candies in my bag. "Thank you."

She nodded and lifted her sandwich to her mouth, then set it down. "I have to tell you something I heard at the store yesterday."

Betty often helped out at the general store. Sometimes, if she was quiet while tidying up, the adults would forget she was there. Then she'd hear things meant for the grown-ups only.

"What did you hear?" I asked, taking a bite of my sandwich.

Betty leaned in. "Miss Smith told Dad that Mr. and Mrs. Pearlman left town yesterday in the dead of night," she said. "The bank foreclosed on their house."

"Foreclosed?" My forehead wrinkled. "What does that mean?"

"The bank took the house from them," Betty explained.

My heart stuttered. "Can banks do that?" I asked.

Betty kicked her feet and looked away. "Dad says the Great Depression's getting worse. That's why banks are taking houses."

Worry gnawed my insides. *If Pa's potato crop doesn't flourish, will the bank take our home too?*

"I still don't understand what the Great Depression means exactly. Did you ask your dad about it again?" I said.

Betty and I had both tried asking our parents before, but all they would say was that we shouldn't worry our heads over adult matters.

Betty blew out a frustrated breath. "Dad said something bad happened on Wall Street with the companies. They lost all their money, and so did the people who put their money into those companies."

"I don't understand," I said. "What does that have to do with us?"

"The Depression has everyone in trouble," Betty continued. "Farmers can't sell their crops. Folks are losing their homes. There's a bunch of unpaid bills at the store. Dad tries to give people time to pay but"—she shook her head—"they don't have money. Things are getting worse."

The way she said it made my palms clammy. I thought about the way she'd pushed the caramels into my hand.

"But you're doing all right . . . right?" I asked. "You and your dad are okay?"

Betty turned away.

"Betty?" I whispered.

When she looked back, there were tears in her eyes. "We're not doing well."

"Neither are we." I took her hand. "We'll get through this together."

Betty pulled away. "No, we won't, Millie. Those bank foreclosures I was talking about? It's not just for houses." She sobbed the words. "They took our store and our home. We have nothing left.

Dad says he's closing down the store. We're moving to California."

The ground felt like it was tilting beneath me. "Moving?" I could hardly get the word out. "When?"

"In a few days," she said.

"A few days!" I gripped the edge of the bench tightly. "But you have to pack and close up the store—"

Betty wiped her eyes. "There's nothing to pack up. The bank's taking everything. We don't know where we'll end up. We're taking some clothes and that's it."

I opened my mouth to say something, but all I could do was cry. Betty hugged me, and I hugged her back.

Having my best friend around had made things bearable. Now she was leaving, and I didn't know if I'd ever see her again.

I clung to Betty and cried. Slowly but surely,

I was losing everything that was important to me.

A week later, I walked home alone. Betty and

her father had left town, heading for California,

along with two other families who'd been forced

to abandon their homes.

Everything was getting worse—including the

fights between my parents. Pa kept saying we should

stay, that the rains would come. But like Ma, I knew

we should leave. Only, I couldn't find the words to

say so. Even if I *had* the words, I didn't have the

courage.

As I walked along the road, a change crackled

around me. The air turned dry and staticky and set

my heart racing. Another storm was coming.

I spun, trying not to panic, and looked for shelter. There was no place to hide. Everything was open.

Think, Millie, think!

I couldn't run. Dust storms could block the sun and turn day into night. People had gotten lost—or worse—because they couldn't see their way.

Staying on the side of the road was equally dangerous. If a car came my way and the driver couldn't see me in the storm, I'd get hit.

The wind hummed with the impending storm. I was out of time. There was only one thing I could do. I jumped into a ditch, got on my hands and knees, and hunkered down.

The storm hit, blasting me with sand and dirt. Pebbles pinged off my body. Broken brambles and pieces of tumbleweeds battered my skin.

The wind screamed, and in the distance, a car horn blared. Tires squealed.

I bolted upright, my body tensed to run, and blinked hard, squinting to spot the vehicle. Another blare of the horn, then the sickening crunch of metal crashing into something.

I stumbled back and landed in the dirt. My lungs burned. I squeezed my eyes shut tight, but tears leaked out, mixing with dirt and turning to mud. The cuts on my face and arms stung from the dust and tears.

I curled into a ball as the storm raged on. All I wanted was for things to go back to normal, when the fields grew crops and the rain fell. I missed the feeling of clean sheets on my skin. I missed being outside without being afraid.

Dirt swept alongside me, and I pressed my face into my thighs. The dirt blew, higher and higher, until I was sure it was going to bury me alive.

CHAPTER FOUR

Finally, the dust died down. It hadn't buried me, but it had come halfway up my body.

I pulled myself to my feet and shook my head, trying to get the debris out of my hair. Then I checked my arms and legs. They were covered in scratches, and I was bleeding in a few spots from the branches hitting me.

I scanned the rest of my body, amazed I had been so lucky—this time. But the storms would come again. What if next time, there was no ditch to hide in? What if the next storm was worse than this one?

I shivered at the dark future and stumbled home. When I turned onto the farm, I spotted Ma running down the dirt road.

"Millie!" she screamed. Her dress flapped around her legs as she raced toward me.

"Ma!" Tears burned my eyes, but I blinked them away.

She gathered me tightly in her arms. "I was so worried!"

"I'm okay," I hiccupped.

She pulled away to arms' length. "You're covered in dirt."

"I'm always covered in dirt." I tried to laugh as I said it, but Ma only frowned.

She reached for me again, and I stepped back. "No, Ma, I'm dirty and bloody—" I started to protest.

"I don't care," she said, hugging me tightly.
"I just don't care."

The love in her voice undid me. What if I hadn't made it through the storm? What if I never got to hug my ma again?

The tears welled up. This time, I didn't stop them.

Cimarron County (No Man's Land), Oklahoma
Horn family farm
Monday, April 8, 1935
7:30 p.m.

While Ma got supper on the table, I took a long bath. The soap made my cuts sting, but I took it. Bathing was the only time I felt clean.

I dressed, then heard my folks arguing downstairs. Quietly, I pulled open my door and listened.

"Those blasted storms!" said Pa, his voice raw with frustration. "This one's nearly obliterated the crops. I'll have to dig and see if I can save any of the plants. We'll be lucky to get enough potatoes for ourselves, let alone to sell."

"Sell?" Ma repeated, her voice hitching high. "Who will buy our potatoes? Who has the money? Last year, we couldn't even get proper payment for the wheat! Things are worse this year!"

"Potatoes are a staple. Everyone loves them," Pa said. "Prices'll go back up again. It was just a few years ago that wheat was selling for more than a dollar a bushel."

Ma sighed. "That was during the war. The government needed crops to feed our soldiers. There's no war now and the Depression—"

"The Depression can go to tarnation!" Pa spat out. "Worry about next year's crops. I'm thinking turnips. I've heard they're hardier."

"Hardier!" Ma was like a snake about to strike. "What about your daughter? You think she's hardy enough to survive getting trapped outside during another storm?"

"Course she is. She's a Horn, ain't she?" Pa said.

"She could have been hurt," Ma said. "Like that poor boy who got caught in the barbed-wired fence." Her voice hitched. "Or worse."

The memory of the storm burrowed into my mind. In an instant, I was back there. I could feel the wind and smell of the dust clogging my nose.

Breathing hard, I pushed my fist against my chest and tried to fight back the terror. Instead, all I got was a painful pounding in my temples and a rushing in my ears.

"Nonsense," said Pa. "Millie's smart as a whip! She got herself out of harm's way. She's capable and strong. Don't worry about her. Worry about next year's crops."

"Crops! You're talking about crops when you should be talking about moving!" Ma cried.

"We're not leaving the farm." Pa's voice went rough with frustration. "We need to have something to pass on to Millie."

"There's nothing to pass on, John!" said Ma. "Everyone's leaving, and so are opportunities. What'll be left for Millie when she's grown? A ghost town!"

"That won't happen, I promise," he said. "Next year—"

"You and your promises," Ma said bitterly. "It's like the farm is worth more than your wife and daughter."

My heart hammered so hard I thought it would explode. I couldn't stand it any longer. Even if I got in trouble for eavesdropping, I had to say something.

I ran down the stairs and stumbled to a stop in front of my folks. The noise in my ears thundered. I didn't want to cause more trouble by making it seem like I was picking sides, but I had to speak up.

"Ma's right," I said, barely hearing my own voice. "We need to leave."

Ma nodded and gave Pa a fierce look.

"You're just a child," Pa said. "You don't understand—"

"I understand enough," I said. "I understand that the crops aren't selling and my best friend is gone and Mr. Johnson died from dust pneumonia."

I clenched my insides and said the thing that scared me most. "What happens if you and Ma die from the dust pneumonia? What if I lose you?"

The image of finding my folks' lifeless bodies in the fields rose in my mind. Tears fell hard and fast, cascading down my cheeks.

Ma knelt beside me. "You wouldn't be alone. We have relatives in Texas who would take you in."

"I don't want relatives!" I cried. "I want you." I clung to Pa. "Please, listen to us. We're never clean, no matter how hard we try. There's always

dirt on us. There's dirt everywhere—in our beds, on the tables, in our food. I see you working all the time and for nothing." My voice shook. "I love this place too, Pa, but we have to go."

Pa stared at Ma and me. After a long minute, he turned on his heel and walked away.

I turned and ran to my room. There, I pulled the covers over my head, listened to the sound of dirt falling on the floor, and hated every second of it.

Cimarron County (No Man's Land), Oklahoma
Horn family farm
Tuesday, April 9, 1935
6:50 a.m.

The next morning, I woke to puffy eyes and a headache. Quiet voices drifted from outside. On the porch steps, Ma and Pa stood, looking into the field. The floorboards squeaked beneath me, and Pa turned.

"Millie, my girl," he said, "we're leaving. You and your ma are right. Time to put the money toward the move instead of another year's crops."

My heart skipped with happiness then stuttered to a stop. There was no quiet calm in Pa's voice, just resignation.

Part of me wanted to ignore Pa feelings. He was doing what Ma and I wanted. But he was my pa. He'd always cared about my feelings. I couldn't stop caring about his.

"Are you sure?" I asked.

Pa nodded curtly. "The land's the past. You are the future. We have to do what's right by you." He put his hand on the top of my head. "You're about to become a California girl," he said with a smile. Only, the smile didn't reach his eyes.

I worried about the lifelessness in his voice. But I shook it off. I'd stood up to Pa. Now he was doing what was right for us.

I hugged Pa. His arms stayed at his sides. "Pa?"

Pa put his arms around me and patted my back, but it felt empty. There wasn't the usual love in his embrace.

"Better see if anyone might want to buy this farm," Pa said, pulling away from me. "There's a good girl."

He turned and walked away. Normal times, he'd always look back at me and wink. This time, he kept walking.

Worry crept back in. I took a breath and quieted my thoughts. We were doing the right thing. We needed to leave the farm. Pa might be sad now, but soon he'd see that moving to California was the right thing to do.

Things will get better now, I told myself. They had to.

CHAPTER FIVE

Cimarron County (No Man's Land), Oklahoma
Horn family farm
Sunday, April 14, 1935
10:53 a.m.

Despite Pa's promises, the next weekend, we were no closer to leaving. Sunday morning came with achingly blue skies and white clouds.

I stood in the sunshine, feeling the warmth on my bare arms. If I closed my eyes, I could almost pretend it was a different time—five years ago, when the rain fell and our wheat grew.

Creaking on the porch's boards brought me back to the present. Pa stood there, smiling into the sunshine.

"Perfect day for a picnic, don't you think?" he asked.

I hesitated. "We should pack."

"Ah, packing can wait a couple of hours," he said with a wave of his hand.

"What about packing?" Ma asked, stepping from the kitchen and onto the porch. She wiped her wet hands on a checkered dish towel.

"We'll pack after a picnic," Pa said.

Ma frowned. "You've been promising to help pack for days. We can't keep putting off the move."

"No one's putting off anything," Pa said, the words coming out clipped. "I've just been busy sorting things with the bank."

"The bank?" I said. "What is there to sort out with the bank?"

Ma glanced at me. "We haven't been able to find anyone willing to buy the farm. The bank is going to be taking over."

An emptiness filled my belly. I knew what "taking over" really meant. Foreclosure. Just like with Betty's house and the general store.

Pa pursed his lips. I knew the idea of the bank taking over his family's farm was eating at him.

"One more day in the Oklahoma air," he said. "Then I'll get us sorted for California."

The edges of his lips turned down at the last word, as if he couldn't bear to speak it.

Ma nodded, but her eyebrows pulled together. After a week of Pa's promises, I could tell she didn't quite believe him.

There was a sour feeling curdling in my stomach, but I ignored it. "Picnic and then packing," I said, forcing a smile.

I went inside and helped Ma pack our lunch. We put everything into the car and drove to a scenic spot to eat. Soon we were far from the homestead, sitting on a blanket and eating sandwiches.

Pa set down his food, tilted his head back, and inhaled. "Is there anything better than this?" he asked.

Ma sighed contentedly. "No, there isn't." She smiled at me and stroked my hair. "Almost like old times, huh?"

Ma turned her face to the sun and lay down. Soon, her breathing turned slow and relaxed.

Pa grinned. "Hope she doesn't start snoring," he whispered. He settled next to her and closed his eyes. "There's nothing like home, Millie. Nothing like Oklahoma soil and sun."

While my folks napped, I looked for flowers. All I found were dozens of rabbits. In the past few years, their numbers had grown. They could overrun a farm and destroy crops.

I understood why farmers thought of them as pests, but I felt bad for the animals. They were like us, struggling to survive.

Ahead of me, one of the rabbits lifted its head and sniffed the air, then turned and ran. The others followed.

I laughed. "I don't smell that bad!" I called after them.

A few minutes later, I shivered. The temperature was dropping. I rubbed my arms and flexed my fingers, hoping to get warmth back into them.

Is this what made the rabbits flee? I wondered. Then it hit me. *The animals must know something is about to happen.*

My skin turned colder but not from the weather. I ran back to my folks.

"Pa! Ma! Wake up!" I hollered.

The noise I made woke Ma. "Millie, what is it?" she asked.

"The rabbits are running away," I said.

"Good," said Pa, keeping his eyes closed. "Those critters can keep running."

"No, it wasn't normal. Something about it felt wrong—" The words died on my lips as I saw what was over Ma's shoulder.

Ma frowned at me, then looked behind her. She cried out and stumbled to her feet.

"John!" She pushed Pa's shoulder. "Millie, get everything in the basket. Now!"

I wanted to obey, but my body was frozen. My gaze was fixed on the horizon. The bright-blue sky had been halved by a large, rolling cloud of black. Its length ran the entire horizon. The cloud raced along the ground, coming faster than I thought anything could move.

Above it were flocks of birds, trying to fly away. But the cloud was growing higher. I was losing sight of the birds.

"What's the—?" Pa opened his eyes and followed our gaze. His skin blanched. "Get in the car, Millie," he said tightly.

My feet were rooted. My eyes were fixed on a billowing cloud of dust.

"Now!" yelled Pa.

I jumped, then turned and started running.

"Mary!" I heard Pa call from behind me. "Forget the blankets and baskets! Run!"

I stumbled into our car, my shins slamming against the metal frame. Pain shot through my body, but I ignored it and clambered inside.

I watched through the windows as the cloud raced to my parents. The sky got darker and darker. Ma and Pa dove into the car.

"What's happening?" I had to yell to be heard above the wind.

Ma didn't answer. She bent down, and I heard fabric tearing, then the sound of water being poured.

"Put this over your head," Ma said, handing me a patch torn from her skirt. "Get down and curl into a ball!"

I did what she said, but the cloth covering my face felt like it was suffocating me. My chest ached, and I couldn't breathe.

I ripped the fabric off, trying to get oxygen into my lungs, but the air was full of dust and sand. It clogged my nose and set me coughing.

"Millie! Get that cloth over your face now!" Pa roared. His voice—full of panic and fear and anger—was one I'd never heard before.

I tried to cover my face, but my hands were shaking. Pa started up the car.

"Where are you going?" Ma asked. "It's dangerous to drive!"

"It's more dangerous to stay!" Pa said.

The wind rocked the car from side to side, and the headlights flickered on and off.

"What the—?" Pa said. "It's the dang static electricity!"

Seconds later, the engine died.

"It'll be fine, you hear, Millie? We'll get through—"

Before Pa could finish, the cloud hit, and everything went black.

In the dark, a hand tapped at the seat, trying to find me. I reached out, fumbling, and found Ma's fingers. I gripped them tightly.

There was a thump as something hit the roof. Then another thump and another.

"Oh, Lord," Ma moaned, tears in her words. "It's the birds. They're falling out of the sky." She wept and prayed.

"It'll be fine," Pa kept repeating. "It'll be okay."

He didn't believe it. I heard it in his voice, and I understood the terrible truth. It was the end of the world, and none of us were going to survive.

CHAPTER SIX

The world didn't end that Sunday, but for a lot of people, it ended their world.

Folks, lost in the pitch black, died just steps from their homes. Farm animals and wildlife fell to the storm.

On the radio, the announcer reported the storm was a thousand miles long. He said there had been winds up to a hundred miles an hour. Sailors in the Atlantic Ocean, clear across the country from us, had found a quarter-inch of dust on their ship decks.

Something broke between Ma and Pa that day too. When the storm was over, we were forced to walk home because the engine wouldn't start. Ma didn't speak the whole way.

I knew what she was thinking. If we had left when she'd wanted to, we would've been in California already.

Wednesday afternoon, I stood beside our car, watching as Pa cinched our belongings onto the roof of our car. We weren't taking everything, just enough clothes and food to get us to California.

Ma stepped outside. Pa gave her an unsure smile. She didn't smile back.

I glanced at Pa. His eyes misted as he looked at the farmhouse.

"I'm sorry, Pa," I said quietly. "I know it's hard to give up the farm."

Ma came closer. Hearing my words, sympathy softened her eyes.

"That storm," Pa said. "Hearing those birds fall from the sky—" His skin paled. "It's best to leave 'afore things get worse."

Ma stepped toward the passenger-side door. Pa opened it and held out his hand. She took it, and the tight, cold ball inside me thawed.

When Pa drove from the farm, though, sadness overwhelmed me. This had been the only home I'd ever known. Now it was gone. We were doing the right thing, but it was breaking my heart.

At the edge of town, Pa stopped to fill up the gas tank. There were two men standing near the pump.

"They're saying the wind went as far as the nation's capital," the gray-haired one said. "I was riding my horse home in it. The static electricity was so bad, it was setting the cow chips on fire."

The short man next to him whistled. "The storms are hitting everywhere now."

Ma gave me an anxious smile. "It's going to be okay, honey. We're heading out to California. Things will get better. You'll see."

She smiled wider when Pa climbed back in. "All set?" she asked.

Pa turned to face her. "We sure about this move? What if we get to California and the dust follows? We'll be in the same situation as before, except without a house or a way to feed ourselves."

"Did the storms hit California?" Ma asked.

"Well . . . no," said Pa. "As far as I know, it was Colorado, Kansas, Texas, Oklahoma, Washington, and maybe New York."

"Then we're fine," said Ma. "We've talked about this. It's time to move. The house has gone back to the bank. We don't have a home here anymore."

Pa's eyes watered as Ma nodded at the wheel. "Let's get going."

We headed out. The days were long and tiring. Now that we were on our way, Pa wanted us in California as fast as possible. He drove two hundred miles a day. To make our money last, we parked behind billboards and slept in the car. We only ate once a day.

It was hard, but I told myself we were doing what was needed. Things would be better in California. They had to be.

Traveling to Antioch, California
Wednesday, April 24, 1935
5:53 p.m.

As we drove, the scenery changed. Barren fields and brown landscape shifted to green trees and lush crops. Finally we drove past a sign that read WELCOME TO CALIFORNIA.

I clutched my hands together in excitement. I didn't blink—I wanted to see and feel everything.

We were here, and things were finally going to get better. There wouldn't be dirt or storms. We'd find a home and there would be food.

Ma reached back and squeezed my hand. "Time for a new adventure," she said.

But as we drove farther, my hope dimmed. Ramshackle tents lined the road. I saw homes built of cardboard, some of tin, others of crates.

None of them looked fit to keep folks warm or safe from the elements.

Traffic slowed and gave me a chance to scan the people living in the broken-down houses. I cringed as a woman dipped a bucket into the ditch water, then poured it into a pot sitting on top of a fire.

"Ma?" I asked hesitantly. "What's that lady doing with the water?"

"Don't fret about it, honey."

I kept watching the lady. She added potatoes to the water.

She's using ditch water to cook her meal,
I realized in horror.

Pa saw her too. His mouth pulled into a tight, hard line, and he didn't say anything.

"Everything will be fine," Ma insisted.

The numbers of tents and people living in ditches increased the closer we got to Antioch. When we arrived at the city limits, there was a car in front of us. A police officer stood by the driver's door.

Pa put down his window. So did Ma.

"Go back home," the cop said to the driver in front of us. "No one wants you Okies here."

"We're not from Oklahoma!" the driver said. "We're from Nebraska."

The cop smirked. "All of you are Okies to us, and Okies don't get in."

My stomach twisted. We were from Oklahoma. *Will the cops refuse to let us into the city? What will we do if we aren't allowed in?*

I looked over at Pa, but he was as still as stone.

Ahead of us, the driver got out of his car. A woman got out of the passenger seat too. Worry and fear lined her face.

The cop's mouth twisted as he faced the couple. "Get out of here," he growled.

"I told you," said the man, "my wife and I aren't from Oklahoma."

"And *I* told *you* that anyone from the Dust Bowl is an Okie to us," the cop spat. "Okies bring disease. You're not welcome here. Go back where you came from."

The woman began to cry.

"We don't have money to get back home," said the man. His voice shook with rage.

"That's not my problem," said the cop. "Go stay with your own kind—in the ditches, where you bums belong." He took out his baton and spun it in a circle. "Now get before I make you go."

Without another word, the man turned and helped the woman into her seat, then went around to the driver's door and climbed in. He put his car in gear and drove toward the ramshackle homes.

"I'm sorry," Ma whispered to Pa. "I thought it would be better here."

Pa stared at the tents. "In Oklahoma, we had a house. I gave up my family's land for nothing," he bit out. "There's no money to go back. We're trapped here."

Just then the police officer started toward us. I shrank in my seat.

"More of you?" the cop said with a sneer.

"I heard what you told the other people," said Pa. "I just want to get into town and get some supplies for my family."

The officer squinted at the darkening sky. "We don't like your kind in our town after nightfall. You cause trouble." He nodded at the

tents. "See that shantytown? That looks about right for you folks."

My body flashed hot, then cold. I wanted to shout at him, to tell him that he had no right to talk to my pa that way. He had no right to say that about folks from anywhere! We'd lost our homes. All we wanted was a chance to make our lives better.

I expected Pa to say something. But instead of arguing, he swung the car around and drove back toward the makeshift town.

The ball of ice that had been thawing inside me since we left our farm refroze. If Pa wasn't standing up for us, then things were worse than I feared.

Pa pulled over on the side of the road, behind a line of cars, and parked.

"We'll have to find food and shelter tomorrow," he said. "For now, it'll be another night of sleeping in the vehicle."

Ma reached out, but Pa moved away. "I should see about food," he said gruffly.

"It's fine," Ma said. "We're not that hungry." She turned to face me. Unshed tears were in her eyes. She gave me a trembling smile. "Are we, Millie?"

I shook my head. "No, Ma. Not at all."

It was true. I wasn't hungry—I was sick to my stomach.

"Fine," said Pa. "Let's try to get some shut-eye."

I curled up, facing the rear of the car. I was terrified we had made things worse. We'd left Oklahoma to get away from the dirt. Now, it seemed, we'd be living in it.

CHAPTER SEVEN

Antioch, California
City limits
Thursday, April 25, 1935
8:19 a.m.

The next morning, I woke with a thumping headache and a growling belly.

Ma smiled. "Morning, sunshine. Let's get up and at 'em."

I rubbed my eyes. "Where's Pa?"

Her smile faltered. "He got up early and went exploring. Just like we should do."

Ma and I walked the short distance from the side of the road to the shantytown.

"Welcome to Hooverville!" a round-faced man by a fire called.

I frowned. "Hooverville?"

Ma hushed me. "It's a joke the adults have. They blame President Hoover for plunging us into the Great Depression and losing folks their homes."

The man waved us over. "Saw you arrive yesterday. Name's Ralph." He held out his hand.

"My name's Mary," said Ma, shaking his hand. "This is Millie." She put her hand on my shoulder.

"Welcome to my fine abode," said Ralph. "You folks hungry?"

"Oh no." Ma said. "We're fine."

Just then, my belly growled, long and loud.

Ralph tipped his head back and laughed. "Lemme feed you. Times are hard. They're less hard when we stick together."

"Thank you kindly," said Ma. "We'll find a way to pay you back."

Ralph waved away the words. "Had a little girl, just about your age," he said to me. "She and her mother died from the dust storms." He blinked fast. "I'd like to think if it'd been me that passed, folks would've helped them."

We sat around the fire while Ralph shared his bread and coffee. I swallowed the bitter brew and coughed.

"Sorry, Millie. Coffee's the best we got around here." Ralph shook his head. "It tastes like ditch water, but it's all I can offer."

I forced myself to take another sip. "It's good, sir," I said. "Thank you."

After we ate, Ma gave me permission to explore. I wandered through the maze of houses, mindful of where I stepped.

I kept my distance out of respect, but also caution. There were no streets or paths. The homes had been built anywhere there was space. Most of them slanted to one side or the other, and I worried touching them might bring the walls down.

I tried not to think of our farmhouse back in Oklahoma. It would only make me cry.

As I turned left through the cluster of homes, a group of folks caught my attention. There were ten or fifteen adults sitting around. Kids ran in between them, playing games and laughing.

Just then, the crowd parted, and in the space, I saw Pa. I pressed my hands against my mouth when I saw who he was sitting with—Mr. Adams and Betty!

"Betty!" I shouted.

My best friend jumped up, then raced to me. I grabbed her in a tight hug.

Betty was sobbing. "Millie! I didn't think I'd ever see you again! Everybody's been talking about that terrible storm that hit Oklahoma and the other states. They're calling it Black Sunday because of how dark it got." She wiped her tears. "I'm so glad you're okay!"

I pulled back and looked at my friend. She was thinner than the last time I'd seen her. Worry mixed with my happiness.

"Why are you here?" I asked. Betty and her father had left Oklahoma weeks ago. "Don't you—don't you have a house?"

The light in Betty's eyes faded and she shook her head. "It's terrible here. The city folks hate us. They think we're dirty and diseased. They think we're going to steal their jobs."

She pulled a flyer from her pocket. "But folks come here because they're told there are jobs."

I took the paper from her hand and read the words: PICKERS WANTED! WORK IN CALIFORNIA! GOOD WAGES! COME AT ONCE!

"They say they want folks to come and work," Betty said, "then hate us for doing it!" Tears spilled down her cheeks. "Plus, there're more workers than work. The farm owners know we're desperate, so they lie. They say they'll pay one wage at the end of the day. Then, when the day ends, they pay us less."

"Us?" I asked.

"Even the kids are working." Betty laughed harshly. "I worked with Pa for twelve hours, and all they paid us was a dollar and twenty-five cents. That's not enough to do anything."

I squeezed her hand. Then I saw Pa watching and realized he'd heard it all. He came toward me.

"What'll we do, Pa?" I asked.

"There's nothing to do but make do," he said. "I'll talk to your ma. We'll do what we need so we can survive."

"I'll help too," I said. "I can be a picker!"

"No." Pa's face went tight. "I don't want you out in these conditions. It's backbreaking work. I'll not have you be part of it. We'll get you into school."

"Good luck," said a man standing close by. "Try to find a school that'll take a migrant kid."

Pa's face closed in.

"I want to help," I insisted. "We're family, and we stick together."

Pa's expression stayed hard. "I said no, Millie, and I meant it. Don't sass me." His stern words shocked me into silence. "Let's find Ma. We've got to head into the city and get supplies."

"Be careful," Betty said, her voice low so Pa wouldn't hear. "Some of the folks in the city are beating up anyone from the shantytown."

"I'll be careful," I said, trying to sound brave and failing miserably.

Antioch, California
Owens' General Goods Store
Thursday, April 25, 1935
9:29 a.m.

My folks and I drove into town for supplies. There were no officers around to stop us, but the relief I felt at that realization died as we drove the city streets.

Folks glared in our direction. "Go home!" they shouted.

I shrank in my seat, pretending not to notice. Pa noticed, though. The muscles in his jaw bulged as he clenched his jaw.

"Happy now?" he said to Ma.

"How could I have known?" Ma replied.

"You should have trusted me!" Pa's grip tightened on the steering wheel, and I flinched at the sharpness in his voice.

"I do trust you," Ma said quietly.

"I can't even do anything about those hooligans," Pa muttered. "It's me they'll put in jail. You heard those cops." His voice went thick. "We're dirty Okies."

Ma blinked back tears and didn't say another word.

Pa parked, and we hurried to the store for groceries. But halfway there, Ma stopped and whirled back. "I left my purse in the car!"

"I'll get it," I said.

"No, I want you close," Ma said.

"It's right there," I told her. "You can see it."

"It's not safe," Pa insisted.

I was desperate to get space from my folks. The anger between them was suffocating me.

"The streets are empty," I said. "I'll be right back." I took the car keys from Pa and hurried away before they could stop me.

I grabbed Ma's purse from the car and turned back toward the store. I hadn't taken more than a few steps when a group of kids surrounded me.

"Give it here, Okie," said the redheaded ringleader.

I clutched the purse tightly and glanced around for help, but I was alone.

"Get away from me," I told him. I tried to sound strong, but my voice came out thin and high. "I don't want no trouble."

The boy laughed. His face fell into hard lines. "Then you should've stayed in your dirty little house."

He lunged for me. I kicked him in the shin, then ran for the store. My heart hammered in my chest, and the sound roared in my ears.

Behind me, the group shouted. Their footsteps came hard and fast, pounding after me. Someone grabbed for me—I felt their fingers graze my shoulder—and I pushed myself harder.

Faster, Millie, faster!

My lungs burned as I sped for the safety of the store, praying I would make it in time.

CHAPTER EIGHT

Pa was already coming my way. The shopkeeper stood outside the door.

"Get!" Pa yelled at the boys.

The fury on his face scared me. It must have scared the bullies too. They slammed to a stop.

The ringleader spit at us, then turned to his group. "Forget it," he said. "They ain't worth much, anyway."

Pa gripped my shoulders and herded me toward the store. "I told you it wasn't safe. You mind me from now on, you hear?"

I nodded.

"Are you happy now?" Pa asked Ma as we followed the shopkeeper inside. "Think Millie's future's looking up?"

"John—" Ma started to say.

Pa ignored her.

The shopkeeper—Mr. Owens, according to the name tag on his chest—folded his arms and glared at us.

"This is a law-abiding city with good people. If you can't be peaceable, my store isn't the place for you."

"Sir," I said, "you don't understand—"

Pa shushed me. His jaw tight, he turned to Mr. Owens. "We apologize for the ruckus. We'll be going soon."

We bought enough food for the night, then headed back to the car. I hurried to catch up to Pa's long strides.

"Pa, what Mr. Owens said isn't right—"

"It don't matter," Pa said. "It's his store.
He can say and do whatever he pleases."

"But those boys tried to steal from us!" I said.

"Don't you get it?" Pa rounded on me. "No one
wants us here."

I jumped at the harshness in his voice. Ma put
her arm around my shoulder.

"You keep your head down," he said. "Stay
quiet and stop causing trouble. You hear?"

I nodded. "Yeah, Pa, I hear."

We drove back to the shantytown in an icy
silence. I was starting to think it would never melt.

Antioch, California, and San Joaquin Valley
Shantytown
Tuesday, May 14, 1935
4:30 a.m.

"Millie," Pa said gruffly. "Time to get
moving."

I sat up. The rectangle of cardboard that served as my bed cracked under my weight. I wrapped my thin blanket around me.

One of the women from the shantytown had given me the once-pale-blue cloth. Now, it was gray and coated with dirt. We tried hard to keep everything clean, but like in Oklahoma, dust got everywhere.

"I'm coming," I replied.

Pa nodded and stepped outside. Thanks to him and Ralph, our "house" was one of the better ones. They'd found discarded sheet metal for the walls and roof. It was sturdier than the cardboard homes, but the wind and rain still got in. When the days were warm, the house turned into a furnace.

I stepped outside and blinked at the sun rising over the grass. There was a time I had loved the sunrise. It used to mean helping Pa in our fields. Now, all it meant was another day of working hard for another farmer and still not making enough money to leave the shantytown.

Pa had tried to keep Ma and me from having to work as pickers, but it proved impossible. All of us had to pitch in. I worked from sunup, picking cotton in the fields. My fingers were raw and calloused, and my back ached so badly, it was hard to stand upright. Every part of me hurt, especially my heart.

We've been here for weeks, and nothing is getting better, I thought.

"Millie!" Pa called sharply. "Let's go!"

Ma was waiting by the car. She and I looked at each other but didn't say anything. Pa was always mad these days.

I wanted to tell him that Black Sunday had been so bad that our crops would never have survived. Chances are, without our crops, we wouldn't have survived either. But Pa was so angry, talking to him felt like spoiling for a fight.

We headed to the farm in silence, collected our bags, and started picking. I turned my face to the sun, hoping the warmth would ease the ache from my shoulders.

But no matter how hot it got, my shoulders ached, and the ice that had formed between Pa and me didn't thaw. I kept my head down and pretended that speaking my mind hadn't made Pa stop loving me.

Antioch, California
Owens' General Goods Store
Wednesday, June 5, 1935
6:18 p.m.

After work, we drove into town for groceries. Our shadows—Ma, Pa, and me—were separate silhouettes moving down the sidewalk. Pa didn't try to hold Ma's hand like he used to do.

I pressed my fist into my stomach. It felt as if there was a hole there, but I couldn't tell if the emptiness was hunger or heartache.

I spotted a group of men standing by the grocery store and pressed my fist harder. Acid churned higher into my throat.

One of the men, young with black hair, whistled at us. "Lookie, it's the bums from the road. Why're you walking? Your junk car break down, Okies?"

"They ain't Okies," said his thin friend. "They're Arkies. Can't you tell from the dull look in their eyes?"

We got closer, and the men continued to call us names. "Bums" and "undesirables."

"Go back home before you bring your diseases to us!" yelled a third man. "Dirty Okies!"

At that, Pa spun to face him, stepping close and fast. His hands curled into fists.

The man's eyes widened and he backpedaled.

Pa caught me watching and jerked away. "Get inside," he snapped at Ma and me.

We hurried into the store under the suspicious eyes of Mr. Owens. We could only afford bread, potatoes, and turnips. Because we didn't have an icebox, we couldn't buy meat or milk.

As we stepped outside, I saw the group of men again. They had a man from the shantytown in their grips. Two of them held him tight, while the third one punched him.

Ma gasped and pulled me close.

Something deep inside me coiled tight and hot. "We need to do something," I protested, pulling free.

Pa gripped my shoulder and pushed me down the sidewalk. "Stay invisible," he said. "That's how we'll stay safe."

I twisted toward Ma. "They're beating him!"

"Pa's right," she said. "We can't bring attention to ourselves."

"But—"

"Enough, Millie," Pa said. "I left the farm to take care of the family. Now it's your turn. Take care of the family by keeping out of things that don't concern you."

His face softened. For a moment, there was a flicker of my old Pa.

"This is how we stay safe," he said quietly. "Let me protect you."

I nodded and followed my parents down the street. But no matter how far away we got, I couldn't push the terrible images of the man being beaten from my mind.

Antioch, California
Shantytown
Wednesday, June 5, 1935
11:03 p.m.

That night, lying on the carboard with dust sweeping across my face, I wondered if I should have stayed quiet.

Pa's words had made me feel guilty. Ma and I were the ones who'd wanted to leave Oklahoma. Now, Pa picked cotton for another man who underpaid him and called us names.

Sleep wouldn't come. I got up and went walking around the shantytown. Under the moonlight, I spotted a group of shadowy figures lingering by Ralph's house.

What are they doing? I wondered. The pit from earlier was back in my stomach.

A second later, the group ran off, and I spotted a glow by one of the walls. It took me a moment to realize what it was.

"Ralph! Fire!" I screamed. I ran toward Ralph's house as it erupted in flames.

CHAPTER NINE

Antioch, California
Shantytown
Wednesday, June 5, 1935
11:04 p.m.

"I'm here!" Ralph's voice sounded behind me.

He put his hand on my shoulder, then ran to save his house. Other folks rushed to put out the fire with water. But the home—made of wood, tar paper, and cardboard—went up like tinder.

"Why?" Ralph cried, tears coursing down his cheeks. The blaze heated the air around us. "Who would do this?"

We both knew the answer. Ralph's house had been set on fire by locals, angry at us migrants for coming to their city.

Ralph hadn't done anything wrong, but that didn't matter to some people. His house had been close to the road, an easy target, and that had been enough for them.

"I'm so sorry," I said, selfishly relieved it hadn't been our house.

Ralph wiped his eyes. "I'm glad my wife and daughter aren't here to see this."

My eyes burned, whether from the smoke or my tears I couldn't tell. My stomach burned too, but from anger.

It was all so unfair! We were just trying to survive, and working hard to do it.

Ma and Pa threaded their way to me. Their faces were smudged with soot. They looked bone-tired, and probably felt worse.

"I'll help you rebuild," Pa said to Ralph. "In the meantime, you'll stay with us. Tomorrow, we'll get supplies."

Ma hugged me. "Good thing you were here. You stopped the fire from spreading. But no more wandering at night without us, hear?"

I nodded, then looked at Pa.

"Get to bed," he said. "There's work tomorrow."

"Yes, sir," I said, then followed him in silence.

Antioch, California
Owens' General Goods Store
Friday, June 28, 1935
6:53 p.m.

The weeks dragged, and things got worse. Men had started taking turns patrolling the shantytown at night. Even that didn't help me sleep. Worry over another fire—and the fear we'd be trapped here forever—kept me awake.

The days of working in the field didn't help, either. My body was always sore.

After work, Pa and I went back to the store for groceries. I spotted Betty and Mr. Adams coming up the sidewalk and moved for the door, but Pa pulled me back.

"You stay here," he said. "Where I can keep an eye on you."

Mr. Adams came inside. He gave a quick nod to Pa but didn't come over. I knew he and Pa both thought migrants gathering in groups put us in line to get harassed.

I watched Betty standing outside in the sunshine and wished I could go to my friend. A group of kids approached her. One of them said something, and Betty's cheeks turned red. The group closed around her.

Something bad is about to happen, I thought. I moved for the exit.

"Millie!" Pa called. "What did I say? Stay here!"

The pounding of my heart was louder than his voice. It was wrong to simply stand by and watch my friend get bullied. It was wrong to allow cruelty to happen without trying to stop it. I wasn't going to let these kids hurt my friend.

Ignoring Pa, I rushed outside and stepped between Betty and the other kids.

"Oh look, another Oakie," sneered a blond boy. He held his nose. "When's the last time you bathed? You stink!" He and his friends laughed.

"Stop it right now!" I said.

"Make me," he dared.

"Make yourself!" I shouted. "If you'd lost your house and moved to Oklahoma, my family and I wouldn't have hurt you the way you hurt us! No one would've!"

A brown-haired girl looked down her nose at me. "If it's so great where you come from, why don't you go back?"

"Because we can't!" I cried. "Do you think we wanted to leave our homes? Our farm was in my

family for generations! But the drought is killing everything! The storms bury people and animals alive!"

The memories reared up and made tears fall, but I didn't care. "We did our best, but we lost everything! Our animals suffocated. Our crops were buried in dust. People died from the dust."

I wiped my face. "You think we don't want to be clean or sleep in a real bed?" I nodded at the girl and her friends. "You make fun of us, but we grew the food you eat. Now we pick crops here, and we don't even get paid properly!"

"That's 'cause you're worth nothing," said the blond boy. "That's not our fault. No one wants you here. Go back home!"

He shoved me—hard. I fell into Betty. The group surged toward us, their fists out and their faces full of hate. I clenched my hands and readied for the fight.

Just then, there were shouts from the direction
of the store. Pa, Mr. Adams, Mr. Owens, and the
other adults raced outside. They stepped in between
us and broke up the fight.

"Next time, *Oakie*," said the girl. She ran down
the street with her friends.

Pa and Mr. Adams turned to face Mr. Owens.
I bristled as I heard Pa start to apologize to him.
Furious, I stormed away from the store.

Helping Betty wasn't the wrong thing to do.
I was sure of it. Why couldn't Pa see that?

CHAPTER TEN

Antioch, California
Friday, June 28, 1935
7:43 p.m.

As we drove home, the silence between Pa and me threatened to send me out of my skin.

"I didn't do anything wrong," I finally burst out. "What those kids were doing was wrong."

Pa took a deep breath. "Trying to solve a problem with violence is always wrong, my girl," he said.

I wanted to argue, but his voice was soft, like back when he loved me.

"So is staying quiet when you see something bad happening," Pa continued. "I didn't apologize for what you *did*. I only wanted to explain what we've gone through in the past few years. I was trying to keep the shopkeeper, Mr. Owens, from banning us from his store."

"I'm sorry," I said. "I didn't mean to get us banned."

"I know," he said. "Mr. Owens and I cleared the air. He heard what you said to those kids." He chuckled. "Half the county heard you—you got your ma's lungs."

I blushed, then laughed.

"I keep telling you to be quiet, but it was *your* voice he heard," he said. "What you said about being clean, sleeping in a real bed, those things hit him hard. Same thing with our animals and neighbors dying in the storms."

Pa was quiet for a minute. "You taught me a lesson, Millie. All migrants are struggling. We've all lost homes and land."

Warmth spread through me and made my fingers tingle. That was my pa, just like he used to be.

"I've been feeling alone, like I had to take care of myself and my family above everyone else," he said. "I wasn't the only one thinking that way, but it was wrong."

I reached over and took Pa's hand. His gentle strength warmed my fingers.

"Our losses make us all family," Pa continued. "We're stronger as a group. I see that now. I won't stand by and let anyone get beaten up anymore. I promise."

"Thank you, Pa," I said.

Pa glanced at me. "Standing up for the right thing can cost a person big-time. Like when you and your ma told me we had to leave the farm. I'm awful sorry about the way I behaved. I love you, my girl."

There was a fluttering in my chest. I pressed my hand against my heart, and for the first time in a long time I felt it beat with hope.

Antioch, California
Saturday, June 29–Tuesday, July 30, 1935

True to his word, Pa started focusing on the future. He told everyone in the shantytown what happened outside the shop that day.

Some folks were upset. They thought I should have stayed quiet. But Pa stood up for me. He argued we were stronger together.

It took some convincing. Eventually, folks promised to help one another if they saw something bad happening.

We didn't stop there. After dinner most nights, Pa, Ma, and I sat in our metal house and began to brainstorm a way out of the shantytown. We were always bone-tired after a day in the fields, but planning for the future had a way of taking the ache from my body.

Soon, Mr. Adams and Betty joined us in coming up with ideas.

"One of the men was saying the government's looking for men to help build roads," said Mr. Adams one night.

"It'll pay better than the picking," said Pa. "I'm going to try for it."

"What else can we do?" Ma said, more to herself than us. She snapped her fingers. "I could see about taking in mending. It'd pay more than working the fields."

"Maybe Mr. Owens might be open to me working at his store," Mr. Adams suggested.

"I bet if we were clever, we could sort out a way to ration our food," Pa said. "Anything we saved, maybe we could put it toward a proper place to stay."

Mr. Adams nodded. "If your family doesn't mind sharing, we could put our money toward that place."

Pa grinned. "That's a mighty fine idea."

The fluttering of hope in my heart became a beating drum. We were going make it, I knew it.

Los Angeles, California
Friday, August 30, 1935

Betty and I sat in the back of Pa's truck, holding hands. I craned forward, trying to see past Ma's shoulder. "Are we there yet?"

"Millie," Ma laughed. "Stop it. We'll get there when we get there."

"Did you hear the government's doing something called the Soil—" Betty wrinkled her nose.

"Soil Conservation Service," said Ma. "They're hoping that with some regulations, like planting trees, the Plains states can reclaim the soil. Folks

can go back to farming." She touched Pa's arm.

"Folks like us."

Pa nodded. "It'll take a few years for the land

to heal, but in the meantime"—he turned down a

narrow street—"this can be home."

At the end of the road, Mr. Adams, Ralph, and

Mr. Owens stood in front of a small house with a

wooden fence. They waved at us.

Betty and I jumped out of the vehicle and ran

over.

"Now," said Mr. Owens as Pa and Ma joined

us, "it's not perfect, but it's better than the

shantytown."

"It's beautiful," Ma said.

Mr. Owens blinked fast. "I wish I could give

you something better. I'm so ashamed of all the

things I thought and said about the migrants.

I can't change the past—"

Mr. Adams patted him on the back. "We make mistakes, then we do better."

Mr. Owens smiled. "You ready to see your new house?"

Pa rubbed his hands. "Let's take a gander."

We stepped inside the house.

"There's no dirt," Ma said, running her finger along the table in disbelief. "Everything is so clean." She put her hand to her chest and began to cry.

Ralph blinked back tears too. "I'm awful grateful you included me."

"You took care of us," said Pa. "Now we take care of you."

"It'll be a tight fit," said Mr. Adams, looking at Betty and me. "You girls okay sharing a room?"

Betty laughed. "Yes!"

"Once fall starts," said Ma, "you girls will be back in school."

"If we work hard and plan right, who knows?" said Pa. "Maybe next year, each family will have their own home."

I let the conversation swirl around me. I was a little worried about heading into a new school, especially since people weren't keen on us migrants. But I wasn't afraid.

Not everyone would be good to me and Betty, but we had our parents, Ralph, Mr. Owens, and each other. Plus, we had all the strength we'd gained the past few years.

No matter what the world—or the weather— would throw at us, I knew we'd always survive.

A NOTE FROM
THE AUTHOR

There are some stories authors research that break their hearts. For me, that was the Dust Bowl. A series of terrible—and preventable—choices contributed to the disaster. Choices such as the United States government pushing the idea of Manifest Destiny—the belief that it was the destiny of the U.S. to expand its territory over all of North America. The introduction of farming techniques that hurt the environment, plus dishonest salesmen telling folks that rain was plentiful in states like Oklahoma, also played a part. Those choices almost destroyed the landscape of Middle America.

For families like Millie's, who had farmed the land for generations, these choices were devastating. They watched as grasslands were destroyed to make way for crops. No grasses or trees meant there were no roots to hold the soil. Severe droughts came in 1931. With nothing to anchor the dirt, the result was the Dust Bowl—one of the largest man-made climate disasters in history. (In 1934, the government would identify the geographic center of the dust storm. It was Cimarron County, Oklahoma—where Millie lived.)

These storms became known as black blizzards— intense dust storms that carried dirt and sand across hundreds of miles. In some cases, the blizzards brought soil from other states, such as Oklahoma, into neighboring ones, such as Kansas. Black Sunday, one of the worst blizzards, occurred on Sunday, April 14, 1935. It caused immense damage to homes and land and resulted in many deaths. More than 300 million tons of topsoil were lost during this storm, which reached as far as Washington, D.C.

It's no wonder that Millie and her ma would have pushed to move west. The other states held hope—for jobs, clean air, and survival. But life wasn't easier in these new places. Locals resented the people who moved to their states from the Midwest. Rumors flew that migrants brought disease and crime. People who moved from the Plains states were harassed and beaten. Migrants, like Millie, were forced to live in shantytowns, and their homes were set ablaze by locals. In 1936, the

Los Angeles police chief launched the Bum Brigade. It employed more than 100 officers tasked with denying migrants entry to California.

Relief, it seemed, would never find those from the Midwest. Thankfully, through government programs, folks were able to regain their independence.

In 1935, President Roosevelt implemented the Works Progress Administration (WPA). The WPA provided paid jobs to help with unemployment. People were hired to build schools and roads. The WPA also sponsored music, plays, and stories by some artists. This program ran for eight years and employed more than eight million people.

The Prairie States Forestry Project also came into effect in 1935. It sought to combat two problems— unemployment and wind erosion. Over the course of seven years, crews planted more than 200 million trees across six states.

Passed on April 27, 1935, the Soil Conservation Service (SCS) was an instrumental program that recognized the dangers of overgrazing and improper farming techniques. It created regulations to prevent soil erosion. It introduced programs that included planting vegetation (plants and trees) to reclaim the land. Farmers learned about sustainable growing techniques and farming procedures that would protect the topsoil.

But people like Millie understood that the true key to surviving hard times wasn't just about independence. It was about *interdependence*. The trick was to ask for help when it was needed and give help when it was asked for. That's why I loved writing about Millie. She embodied the best parts of the people who endured these hard times. Like many of the folks I researched, Millie chose loyalty and helping others over looking out for herself. She stepped in to protect those who were being bullied. Like Pa said, it was *her* voice that Mr. Owens heard.

Millie's story is a powerful reminder that even in the darkest times, our actions and words can bring positive change to the world. Our acts of kindness may feel small, but they live on, through time and history. May you always remember that your kindness can give people hope, that your voice has power, and that this world is better because you are in it.

MAKING CONNECTIONS

1. Pa says repeatedly that his family has owned the land and farm for generations. They've weathered droughts and hard times before. How do you think Pa's connection to the farm influenced how he felt about moving?

2. When Millie and her family move to the shantytown, their structure doesn't have electricity, plumbing, heat, or water. What kinds of things do you think Millie and the other people in the shantytown did to live and survive day to day?

3. In Chapter Ten, Millie says she's worried but not afraid of going to school because her experiences have made her strong. Write a paragraph imagining what Millie's first day at school might be like.

GLOSSARY

abode (uh-BOHD)—the place where someone stays or lives

barren (BA-ruhn)—not producing; unfruitful

bushel (BOOSH-uhl)—a unit for measuring dry goods, such as fruit or grain, that is equal to about 32 quarts (35 liters)

drought (DROUT)—a long period of weather with little or no rainfall

Dust Bowl (DUHST BOHL)—the name given to the region of the United States that suffered from severe drought and dust storms in the 1930s

dust pneumonia (DUHST noo-MOH-nyuh)—an illness unique to the Dust Bowl era, characterized by swelling of the lungs and including chest pain, coughing, and difficulty breathing

foreclose (for-KLOHZ)—to take back property because the money owed for the property has not been paid

gumption (GUHMP-shuhn)—courage and confidence

homestead (HOHM-sted)—a piece of land with room for a home and farm

icebox (AHYS-boks)—refrigerator

jaw (jaw)—to talk for a very long time

migrant (MY-gruhnt)—a person who moves to a new area or country, generally in search of work

migrate (MY-grate)—to move from one place to another

picker (PIHK-er)—a worker hired at the end of the growing season who works the fields, picking crops

ration (RASH-uhn)—the amount of food or supplies allowed by a government

resignation (rez-ig-NAY-shuhn)—the feeling that something unpleasant is going to happen and cannot be changed

shantytown (SHAN-tee-TOWN)—an area of a city where there are many shacks and sometimes no running water or electricity

silhouette (sil-oo-ET)—an outline of something that shows its shape

staple (STAY-puhl)—an important and basic food item that is eaten by most people

Wall Street (WAWL STREET)—a narrow street in New York City, and the first permanent home of the New York Stock Exchange; also refers to U.S. financial institutions as a whole

ABOUT THE AUTHOR

Natasha Deen graduated from college with a psychology degree, but her passion has always revolved around stories. She has written mystery, action, historical, and fantasy novels for kids, teens, and adults. For her, one of the best things about being an author is the chance to slip into other times and worlds, and to be anything she can imagine through her characters. Natasha lives in Edmonton, Alberta, Canada, with her pets and husband. When she's not writing, she spends a lot of time trying to convince her animals that she's the real boss of the house. Visit her at www.natashadeen.com.

photo credit: Richard Jervis

ABOUT THE ILLUSTRATOR

Wendy Tan is a Chinese-Malaysian illustrator based in Kuala Lumpur, Malaysia. Over the past few years, she has contributed to numerous animation productions and advertisements. Now Wendy's passion for storytelling has led her down a new path: children's book illustration. When she's not drawing, Wendy likes to spend time playing with her mixed-breed rescue dog, Lucky.

photo credit: Wendy Tan